The Babe & I

Written by **David A. Adler**   Illustrated by **Terry Widener**

VOYAGER BOOKS   HARCOURT, INC.   *Orlando   Austin   New York   San Diego   Toronto   London*

A NOTE ABOUT THE AUTHOR'S DEDICATION:

I am the second of six children. When my older
brother, Joseph, was a toddler, our aunt Bette
looked at him, laughed, and said, "Hi, Butch."
Joseph laughed, looked at her, and repeated,
"Hi Butch." From then on she has been our
beloved "Hi Butch." I learned from her to
speak lovingly to children, because they repeat
what they hear.

A NOTE ABOUT THE STORY:

While this story is a work of fiction, the newspaper stories of the Coney Island fire, the boy
who robbed a telegraph office, and the reports
of Babe Ruth's home runs, collapse, visit with
the fans in Yankee Stadium, and pinch hitting
appearance are all based on actual events that
were reported July 14 through July 22, 1932.

www.HarcourtBooks.com

First Voyager Books edition 2004
Voyager Books is a trademark of Harcourt, Inc., registered in the
United States of America and/or other jurisdictions.

The Library of Congress has cataloged the hardcover edition as follows:
Adler, David A.
The Babe & I/David A. Adler; illustrated by Terry Widener.
p.   cm.
Summary: While helping his family make ends meet during the
Great Depression by selling newspapers, a boy meets Babe Ruth.
1. Depressions—1929—Juvenile fiction.   [1. Depressions—1929—
Fiction.   2. Moneymaking projects—Fiction.   3. Ruth, Babe,
1895–1948—Fiction.   4. Baseball—Fiction.   5. Fathers and sons—
Fiction.   6. Teamwork (Sports)—Fiction.   7. Unemployment—
Fiction.]   I. Widener, Terry, ill.   II. Title.
PZ7.A2615Bae   1999
[E]—dc21   97-37580
ISBN 0-15-201378-4
ISBN 0-15-205026-4 pb

H G F E D C B

The illustrations in this book were done in
Golden acrylics on Strathmore Bristol board.
The display type was set in Latin Wide.
The text type was set in Cloister Old Style.
Color separations by Bright Arts Graphics Pte. Ltd., Singapore
Printed and bound by Tien Wah Press, Singapore
Production supervision by Sandra Grebenar and Pascha Gerlinger
Designed by Camilla Filancia

For my aunt Bette Adler Guterman,
a baseball fan and our beloved "Hi Butch"
        –D. A. A.

For my wife and children,
whose support makes my work possible
        –T. W.

FOR MY BIRTHDAY I was hoping my parents would give me a bicycle. They only gave me a dime. I was disappointed, but not surprised. It was 1932, in the midst of the Great Depression, and millions of people were out of work. We were lucky. My father had a job. But we never seemed to have much money. Where we lived, in the Bronx, New York, everyone was poor.

"Happy birthday," Dad said when I walked him outside. I watched him go off, carrying his briefcase and smiling.

My neighbor Jacob was tossing a ball and catching it. He threw it to me and shouted, "Give me a high one. I'm Babe Ruth, the world's greatest baseball player."

I threw the ball and Jacob reached up. It bounced out of his hands. He was no Babe Ruth!

We played for a while, and then Jacob said, "I have to go to work. Come with me. We can have a catch while we walk."

A few blocks from home we passed a woman selling apples. Her clothes

were wrinkled and shabby. I gave her my birthday dime and bought two apples, one for me and one for Jacob. I was glad to be rid of the dime. It reminded me of the present I didn't get.

We turned onto Webster Avenue, and there were more apple sellers. Near the next corner I saw a large briefcase. I looked up and there was Dad, selling apples like the others. Suddenly I couldn't move.

"Come on," Jacob said.

I pointed.

"Oh," he whispered, "I thought your dad had a job."

"So did I. And Mom thinks so, too."

There were tears in my eyes as I watched people walk past my father. I wished so much someone would buy an apple from him. But no one did. I realized how he had earned my birthday dime and was sorry I had spent it.

"I have to get to work," Jacob whispered.

I was too dazed to know where we were going. I just followed Jacob until we came to a small building.

"My dad is out of work, too," Jacob said as he got in line. "That's why I'm a newsie. Sell newspapers with me. It's fun."

I didn't feel like going home, so I stayed with Jacob. We collected our papers, and he said, "Now I'll teach you how to really sell."

We walked past a newsie on the corner.
"Coney Island fire," he called out. "One thousand homeless. Read all about it!" There were lots of people around, but I didn't see anyone buy a newspaper.

Jacob and I passed other newsies calling out about the fire. Then
we walked beyond the busy streets and apartment buildings.

"Where are we going?" I asked.

"You'll see," Jacob said.

We walked until we came to an elevated train station. People were rushing from it to the large ballpark just ahead.

"We're here," Jacob said. "That's Yankee Stadium."

I held up one of my newspapers and called out the headline. "Coney Island fire! Read all about it!"

"No," Jacob said. "No one here is interested in fires."

He picked up a newspaper and looked through it. "Here it is," he said. "This is what they want."

"Babe Ruth hits home run!" he called out. "Read all about it! The Babe hits number twenty-five! Read all about it!"

"Here, I'll take one," a man said, and gave Jacob two cents.

"Let me see that," another man said.

Jacob was smart. These people were on their way to see a Yankee game. Of course they were interested in Babe Ruth.

"Babe Ruth hits home run," I called out. "Read all about it."

Jacob and I quickly sold all our papers. When we left the stadium the coins in my pocket made a nice jingling sound.

We went back to the small building and paid a penny for each paper we had sold. That left me with twenty-five cents.

When I got home I didn't tell Mom about Dad and the apples, but I told her about my job. She put the coins I earned in our money jar and said, "Don't say anything to your father about the newspapers. It might embarrass him to know you're helping out."

Later Dad came home and put some coins in the jar. He took off his shoes, stretched out on the couch, and said, "I was really busy at the office today. I'm tired."

I wanted to tell him he didn't have to pretend he still had his job, but I couldn't. I just looked at Dad's briefcase and wondered what he had in there.

The next day Jacob and I called out about Babe Ruth again. He had hit his twenty-sixth home run! I quickly sold my newspapers. I knew I could have sold more, if only I had some way to get them to the stadium.

When I got home I searched the basement of our building for a wagon, or anything with wheels. All I found were boxes and a torn suitcase. Just before I went back upstairs I saw Mrs. Johnson pushing her baby in a carriage.

"Could I borrow that?" I asked.

"Why?" she asked. "You don't have a baby."

I told her about the newspapers.

"I suppose so," Mrs. Johnson said, thinking. "But this would have to be a business arrangement. With my carriage you'll make extra money, so I should make some, too." She offered to rent the carriage to me for ten cents an afternoon, and I agreed.

On Monday the front-page story was about a nineteen-year-old boy who had robbed a telegraph office because he wanted to be arrested. He knew he would get something to eat in jail.

Jacob and I didn't call out about the boy. We called out about Babe Ruth. He had won a game for the Yankees with a hit in the twelfth inning.

Thanks to Mrs. Johnson's carriage, I sold lots of papers. I had eighty cents to give Mom for the money jar.

When Dad came home he gave Mom a bottle of milk and a bag of apples, and said, "I bought the apples from an unemployed man I passed on my way home."

"Dad," I said, "that man is not unemployed. Selling apples is a job."

"No it's not," he said sharply. "It's just what you do while you wait and hope for something better."

He looked upset, and I realized how important it was for him to keep his secret.

On Tuesday Jacob and I called out, "Babe Ruth collapses! Read all about it!" And on Wednesday, "Babe Ruth stays home!" He had hurt his leg, and doctors told him he wouldn't be able to play for three weeks.

That night Dad asked me to walk with him. When we were a few blocks from home he said, "Today I saw you pushing Mrs. Johnson's baby carriage. I spoke with her, and she told me about the newspapers."

"I'm just trying to help, Dad."

He said, "I know."

Dad held my hand firmly. We walked quietly for a while. Then Dad asked, "Were you ever on Webster Avenue?"

"Once."

He squeezed my hand. Tears were rolling down his cheeks.

"I didn't tell Mom," I said.

Dad didn't say anything after that. I didn't either. We just walked.

The next day Jacob and I called out, "Babe Ruth sits with fans! Read all about it!"

"Here, kid. I'll take one." A tall man gave me a five-dollar bill.

"I'm sorry," I told him. "I can't change that."

"That's okay, kid. Keep the change."

I just looked at the money. I couldn't believe anyone would pay that much for a newspaper.

Jacob ran to me. "Do you know who that was?" he asked. "You sold a paper to Babe Ruth."

In the few pictures I had seen of Babe Ruth, he was wearing his baseball uniform. I didn't recognize him without it.

"Wow!" I said. "I just sold a newspaper to Babe Ruth!"

I kept one hand in my pocket, holding on to my Babe Ruth bill. With my other hand I sold newspapers. And I kept looking across the street, toward where Babe Ruth had gone.

When all our papers were sold, I pointed to Yankee Stadium and told Jacob, "I'm going over there." I needed to see Babe Ruth again.

I checked the prices and realized I could buy two tickets and still have plenty left for the money jar. So that's what I did.

The stadium was noisy. Jacob and I walked through a short tunnel and saw a large baseball field. Babe Ruth was in the Yankee dugout with his teammates. When the game started, he stayed there. I guess his leg still hurt.

SECTION 25

I tried to watch everything: the pitcher, the catcher, the batter, the players on the field, and Babe Ruth. Near the end of the game, with the score tied, the Yankee catcher didn't come up to bat. Out came Babe Ruth.

Everyone shouted and waved. I think I cheered the loudest. "He paid for my tickets," I told the man next to us. "He gave me five dollars so I could see the game."

The man smiled.

I think the Red Sox pitcher was afraid Babe Ruth would hit a home run. He purposely threw wide of the plate four times and walked the Babe. We cheered again as Babe Ruth slowly walked to first base. We knew he couldn't hit a home run every time, but at least the Babe was back.

Babe Ruth was part of the 1932 Yankees. That year they were the best team in baseball. He and I were a team, too. His home runs helped me sell newspapers. As I left Yankee Stadium, with the coins I had earned making that nice jingling sound in my pocket, I knew Dad and I were also a team. We were both working to get our family through hard times.